A Note to Parents

DK READERS is a compelling program for beginning readers, designed in conjunction with leading literacy experts, including Dr. Linda Gambrell, Professor of Education at Clemson University. Dr. Gambrell has served as President of the National Reading Conference and the College Reading Association, and has recently been elected to serve as President of the International Reading Association.

Beautiful illustrations and superb full-color photographs combine with engaging, easy-to-read stories and informational texts to offer a fresh approach to each subject in the series. Each DK READER is guaranteed to capture a child's interest while developing his or her reading skills, general knowledge, and love of reading.

The five levels of DK READERS are aimed at different reading abilities, enabling you to choose the books that are exactly right for your child:

Pre-level 1: Learning to read
Level 1: Beginning to read
Level 2: Beginning to read alone
Level 3: Reading alone
Level 4: Proficient readers

The "normal" age at which a child begins to read can be anywhere from three to eight years old. Adult participation through the lower levels is very helpful for providing encouragement, discussing storylines, and sounding out unfamiliar words.

No matter which level you select, you can be sure that you are helping your child learn to read, then read to learn!

Penguin
Random
House

Project Editor Laura Gilbert
Editorial Assistant Anna-Selina Sander
Designer Jon Hall
Senior Slipcase Designer Mark Penfound
Senior DTP Designer Kavita Varma
Producer David Appleyard
Managing Editor Sadie Smith
Managing Art Editor Rob Stobbart
Creative Manager Sarah Harland
Art Director Lisa Lanzarini
Publisher Julie Ferris
Publishing Director Simon Beecroft

Lucasfilm
Executive Editor Jonathan W. Rinzler
Art Director Troy Alders
Continuity Supervisor Leland Chee

Reading Consultant
Linda B. Gambrell, Ph.D.

This American edition published in 2015
First American Edition, 2007
Published in the United States by DK Publishing
345 Hudson Street, New York, New York 10014

Slipcase UI: 002–287414–May/15

Page design copyright © 2015 Dorling Kindersley Limited.
A Penguin Random House Company

© and TM 2015 LUCASFILM LTD.

A catalog record for this book is available
from the Library of Congress.

ISBN: 978-5-0010-1334-1

Printed in China.

www.starwars.com
www.dk.com

DK READERS

BEGINNING
2
TO READ ALONE

STAR WARS
A Queen's Diary

Written by Simon Beecroft

My name is Padmé Amidala.

I am the Queen of my planet.

Today I am going to start a diary.

I am going to start a diary because my life is very busy.

I do not want to forget anything.

My world

If people read this diary in the future, they might not know about my world. So I am going to explain interesting things about my world in these boxes.

Today I tried to count all the rooms in the palace, where I live.

I quickly lost count.

My palace is so large I think I shall never be able to explore all of it.

I love to climb up to one of the
highest rooms.
Then I gaze at the waterfalls that
flow down the side of the mountain.

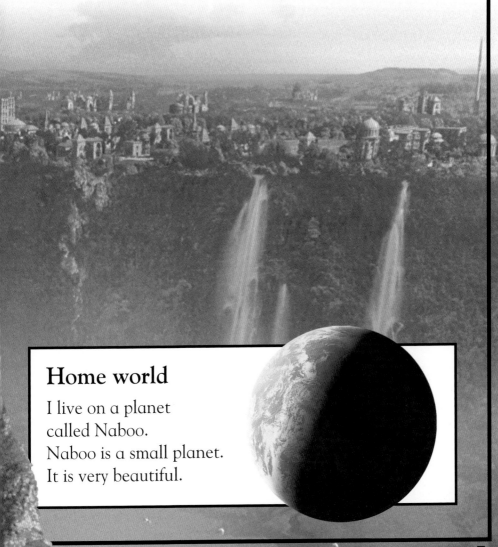

Home world

I live on a planet
called Naboo.
Naboo is a small planet.
It is very beautiful.

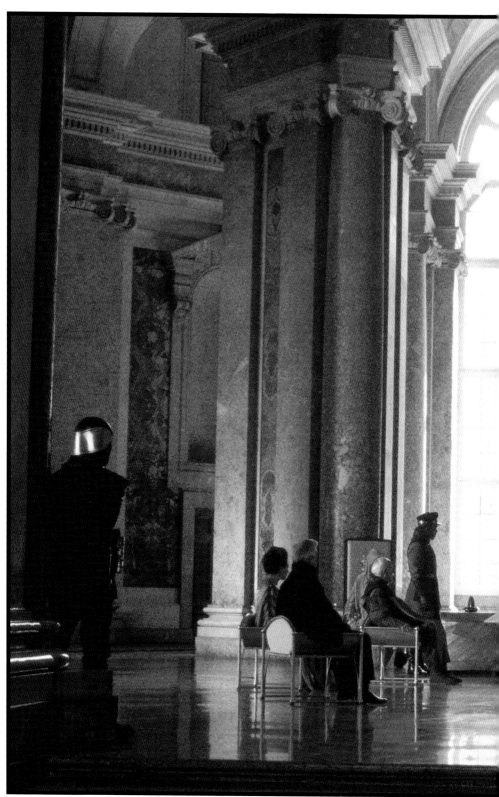

Today a lot of important people
visited me.

When people meet me, some of them
are surprised that I am so young.

I am just 14 years old.

All queens on my planet are young.

I am not even the youngest!

Even though I am not very old,
I want to be a good queen.

Landspeeder

This morning I flew in a landspeeder.
I love travelling fast in landspeeders.
I flew around the city and looked at
all the pretty buildings.
Lots of people waved at me.

My palace is in the biggest city on Naboo, but I have not always lived here.

I was born in a mountain village.

People of Naboo

The humans who live on my planet are called the Naboo. I am one of them. The Naboo live in cities and villages.

I was learning about the Gungans
in my lessons today.
I learned that the Gungans also
live on my planet.
They live in underwater cities.
The Gungans can also live on land.
I would like to meet a Gungan.

Naboo natives

The Naboo and the Gungans do not often meet each other. They are not enemies, but they are not friends either!

Gungan   *Naboo*

I often think about my
parents and sisters.
I have many memories
of growing up
in my village.

When I was young,
my teachers realized
I was very clever.
My teachers gave me
extra training.
Later, people
decided to vote for
me as Queen.
It was the proudest
day of my life!

Padmé

Ruwee

Sola

Jobal

Eirtaé

Rabé

I have handmaidens who look
after me and help me dress.
They also protect me from danger.

My handmaidens are my friends, too.
Eirtaé (pronounced AIR-TAY)
and Rabé are two of my
closest handmaidens.

Royal dress

On my planet,
kings and queens
wear special clothes
and makeup.
They also wear their
hair in special ways.

Today I am going to visit a nearby planet in my special spaceship.

My spaceship is totally silver.

Spaceships

Naboo kings and queens fly silver spaceships. There is even a throne in my ship!

It has large rooms inside.

No one has a spaceship like mine.

I am even learning to fly it.

Sabé

Sometimes it is hard being Queen,
because everyone knows me.
Sabé is my best friend
and one of my handmaidens.

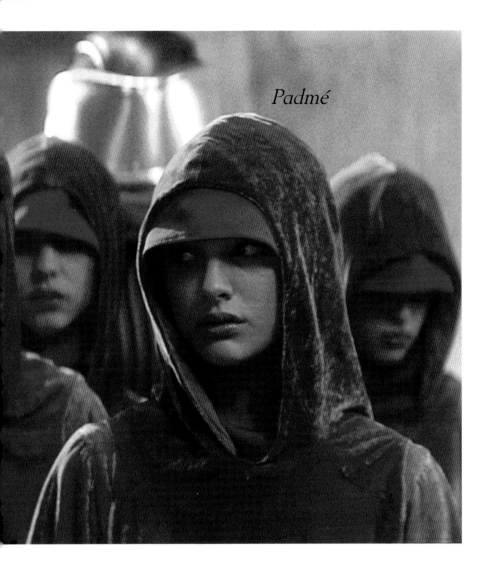

Padmé

Sometimes Sabé dresses as me,
and I dress as a handmaiden.
We have a secret way of talking
in code when we are in disguise.

A terrible thing has happened.

My planet has been invaded.

Enemy soldiers tried to capture me,

but I was saved by two Jedi Knights.

I had never met a Jedi before,

but I had heard about them.

They travel everywhere to help

people in need.

Droid soldiers

The enemy soldiers are machines called droids. Every droid soldier is armed and dangerous.

Now we are flying away from my planet to search for help for my people.

We have landed on a planet
to repair the spaceship.
The planet is rough and dry.
We went to a local town.
I went in disguise so no one
would know I was a queen.
I met a boy who is a slave.
This means that someone
owns him, and he is not free
to ever leave his master.

This young boy is very special.

His name is Anakin.

He told me I looked like an angel.

I think we will be friends.

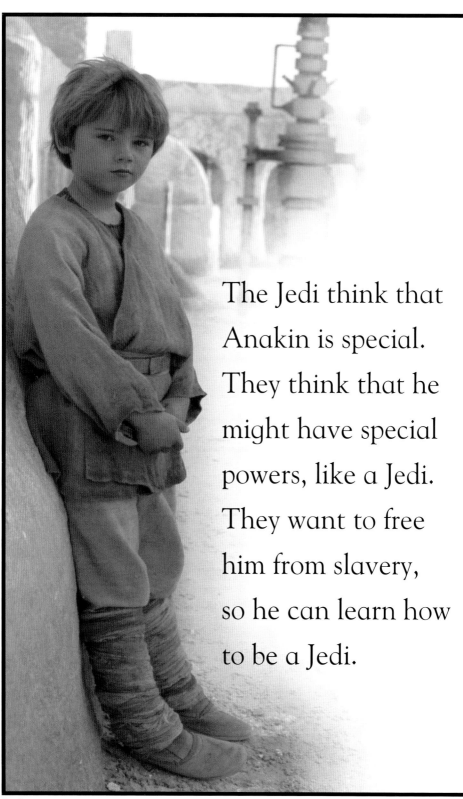

The Jedi think that
Anakin is special.
They think that he
might have special
powers, like a Jedi.
They want to free
him from slavery,
so he can learn how
to be a Jedi.

Amazing news! Anakin is free!
He won a dangerous race in his
Podracer to gain his freedom.
Now we can get help for my planet.

Amazing machines

Anakin has built many clever things.
He built a walking machine called
a droid and a racing machine
called a Podracer.

Droid

Podracer

Today I became a fighter.
No one would help my people,
so I had to help them myself.
I went with the Jedi to ask the
Gungans for help.

Together we made an army
and fought the enemy droid soldiers.
The Gungans fought bravely,
but many of them died.

Weapons

The Gungans use
many weapons in
battle, including
giant catapults.

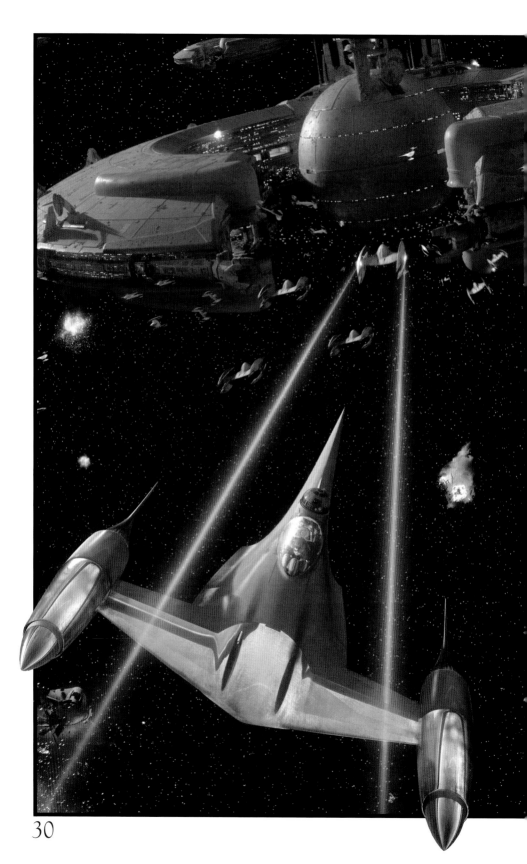

My planet is free!

Anakin helped us a lot.

He flew a spaceship straight into the

invaders' spaceship and blew it up!

Although it was really an accident,

when Anakin destroyed the ship the

droids could no longer fight.

Now I'm sure Anakin

will be trained as a Jedi.

Perhaps we will

meet again....

Places I have visited

I traveled to the swamps on my planet. The Gungans have a secret meeting place there.

I visited a dangerous planet called Tatooine with the Jedi Qui-Gon Jinn. We went to a busy town.

When I was visiting Tatooine, I watched a fast sporting race called a Podrace. A huge crowd gathered to watch the race.

I flew to the center of the galaxy to visit the capital planet. One enormous city covers the entire planet.